KU-104-960

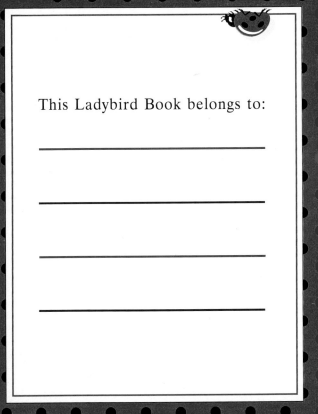

This Ladybird Book belongs to:

_____

_____

_____

_____

All children have a great ambition … to read by themselves.

Through traditional and popular stories, each title in the **Read It Yourself** series introduces children to the most commonly used words in the English language (*Key Words*), plus additional words necessary to tell the story.
The additional words appearing in this book are listed below.

Snow, White, beautiful, queen, magic, mirror, wall, fairest, angry, forest, kill, dwarfs, dead, poison, cloak, bites, falls, prince, picks, piece, poisoned, marry, seven

Ladybird books are widely available, but in case of difficulty may be ordered by post or telephone from:

Ladybird Books – Cash Sales Department
Littlegate Road Paignton Devon TQ3 3BE
Telephone 01803 554761

A catalogue record for this book is available from the British Library

Published by Ladybird Books Ltd Loughborough Leicestershire UK
Ladybird Books Inc Auburn Maine 04210 USA

Snow White
and the
Seven Dwarfs

by Fran Hunia

illustrated by Brian Price Thomas

This is Snow White.

She is a good girl,
and she is beautiful.

Snow White lives with
a beautiful queen.

The queen has
a magic mirror.

She says,
Mirror, mirror, on the wall,
Who is the fairest of us all?

The mirror says,
You are the fairest,
and the queen
is pleased.

One day the queen
looks into her magic mirror
and says,
Mirror, mirror, on the wall,
Who is the fairest of us all?

The mirror says,
Snow White is the fairest.

The queen is angry.

She says to a man,
Take Snow White
into the forest
and kill her.

Snow White and the man
go off into the forest.

Snow White says,
Please do not kill me.
You can say
that you killed me.
I will not go home
to the queen.

Snow White sees
a little white house.

There is no one at home.

She goes in.

Snow White gets
into one
of the little beds.

Seven dwarfs live
in the little house.

They come home and see
Snow White in bed.

Who is this girl?
they say.

Snow White gets up.

She sees the seven dwarfs.

Please help me, she says.
The queen wants to kill me.

You can live here with us,
say the dwarfs.

Snow White thanks
the dwarfs.

The seven dwarfs go off
into the forest to work,
and Snow White works
in the house all day.

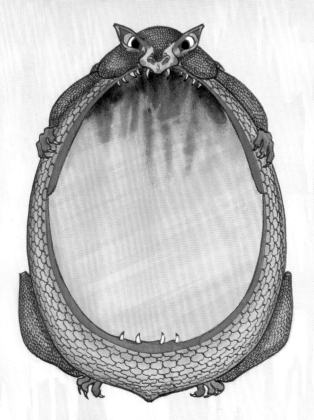

One day the queen
looks into her magic mirror
and says,
Mirror, mirror, on the wall,
Who is the fairest of us all?

The mirror says,
Snow White is the fairest.

What? says the queen.
Snow White is dead.

No, says the mirror.
She lives with seven dwarfs
in a little white house
in the forest.

The queen is angry.

I have to kill Snow White,
she says.

She gets some apples.

The queen puts poison
on the big red apple.

She puts on her black cloak
and goes to look
for Snow White.

The queen sees Snow White
and says,
Here is a big red apple
for you.
Snow White bites the apple.

She falls down
as if she is dead.
The queen is pleased.

The queen goes home
and looks
in her magic mirror.

She says,
Mirror, mirror, on the wall,
Who is the fairest of us all?

You are the fairest,
says the mirror.

The dwarfs come home
and think that Snow White
is dead.

What can we do?
they say.

A prince comes to the house.

He sees Snow White.

What a beautiful girl, he says.

He picks her up, and the piece of poisoned apple falls from her mouth.

Snow White looks at the prince.

The prince says
to Snow White,
Please marry me.

Yes, says Snow White.

She thanks the dwarfs,
and then she goes away
with the prince.

The queen says to her mirror,
Mirror, mirror, on the wall,
Who is the fairest of us all?

Snow White is the fairest,
and she is going to marry
the prince, says the mirror.

The queen is so angry
that she falls down dead.

Snow White and the prince get married.

Everyone is very happy.

LADYBIRD
READING SCHEMES

Read It Yourself links with all Ladybird reading schemes and can be used with any other method of learning to read.

Say the Sounds

Ladybird's **Say the Sounds** graded reading scheme is a *phonics* scheme. It teaches children the sounds of individual letters and letter combinations, enabling them to tackle new words by building them up as a blend of smaller units.

There are 8 titles in this scheme:

1 **Rocket to the jungle**
2 **Frog and the lollipops**
3 **The go-cart race**
4 **Pirate's treasure**
5 **Humpty Dumpty and the robots**
6 **Flying saucer**
7 **Dinosaur rescue**
8 **The accident**

Support material available: Practice Books, Double Cassette pack, Flash Cards